Agua, agüita
Water, Little Water

At Achichipiga At

By / Por
Jorge Tetl Argueta

Illustrations by / Ilustraciones de
Felipe Ugalde Alcántara

Translation by / Traducción de
Gabriela Baeza Ventura

PIÑATA BOOKS

Piñata Books
Arte Público Press
Houston, Texas

Esta edición de *Agua, agüita* ha sido subvencionada en parte por la Ciudad de Houston por medio del Houston Arts Alliance y el Clayton Fund. Les agradecemos su apoyo.

Publication of *Water, Little Water* is funded in part by grants from the City of Houston through the Houston Arts Alliance and the Clayton Fund. We are grateful for their support.

El autor agradece a Genaro Ramirez, María de la Paz Pérez y Paula López, por su ayuda en la traducción al nahuat de este poema "At Achichipiga At", también agradece el apoyo de Carolina Valentina Osorio, Holly Ayala, Alfredo Pérez y José Ardon.

The author thanks Genaro Ramirez, María de La Paz Pérez and Paula López, for their help with the Nahuat translation of this poem "At Achichipiga At;" also many thanks to Carolina Valentina Osorio, Holly Ayala, Alfredo Pérez, Alex Pérez and José Ardon for their support in this project.

¡Piñata Books están llenos de sorpresas!
Piñata Books are full of surprises!

Piñata Books
An Imprint of Arte Público Press
University of Houston
4902 Gulf Fwy, Bldg 19, Rm 100
Houston, Texas 77204-2004

Diseño de la portada por / Cover design by Bryan Dechter

Names: Argueta, Jorge. | Ugalde, Felipe, illustrator.
Title: Agua, Agüita / por Jorge Argueta ; ilustraciones de Felipe Ugalde Alcántara = Water, Little Water / by Jorge Argueta ; illustrations by Felipe Ugalde Alcántara.
Other titles: Water, Little Water
Description: Houston, TX : Piñata Books, an imprint of Arte Público Press, [2017] | Funded by grants from the City of Houston through the Houston Arts Alliance. | Summary: "Describes—in English, Spanish, and Nahuat—the life cycle of water from the perspective of one drop"—Provided by publisher.
Identifiers: LCCN 2017006982 (print) | LCCN 2017007020 (ebook) | ISBN 9781558858541 (alk. paper) | ISBN 9781518504464 (pdf)
Subjects: | CYAC: Water—Fiction. | Polyglot materials.
Classification: LCC PZ10.5.A7 Ag 2017 (print) | LCC PZ10.5.A7 (ebook) | DDC [E]—dc23
LC record available at https://lccn.loc.gov/2017006982

Printed in Hong Kong in May 2017–August 2017
by Book Art Inc. / Paramount Printing Company Limited

7 6 5 4 3 2 1

Para los niños y niñas de El Salvador y del mundo, para que nunca les falte la alegría del agua. Para mi familia pipil-nahua, mis amigos y hermanos y para ti, Abuelita Agua, que eres la vida. En memoria de mi hermano paiute, Lindell Smart.
—JA

Con cariño a mi madre y a la pequeña Catalina.
—FU

For the children of El Salvador and the world, may they always have the happiness of water. For my Pipil-Nahua family, my friends, brothers and sisters, and for you, Abuelita Agua, because you are life. In memory of my Paiute brother, Lindell Smart.
—JA

With love for my mother and little Catalina.
—FU

Mi nombre
es Agua
pero todos
me conocen por "Agüita".

My name
is Water
but everyone
calls me "Little Water."

A mí me gusta
que me llamen
"Agüita".

I like
to be called
"Little Water."

Nazco en el fondo
de nuestra Madre Tierra.
De allá vengo cantando
"Soy gotita".

I am born deep in
our Mother Earth.
From there I come singing
"I am a tiny drop."

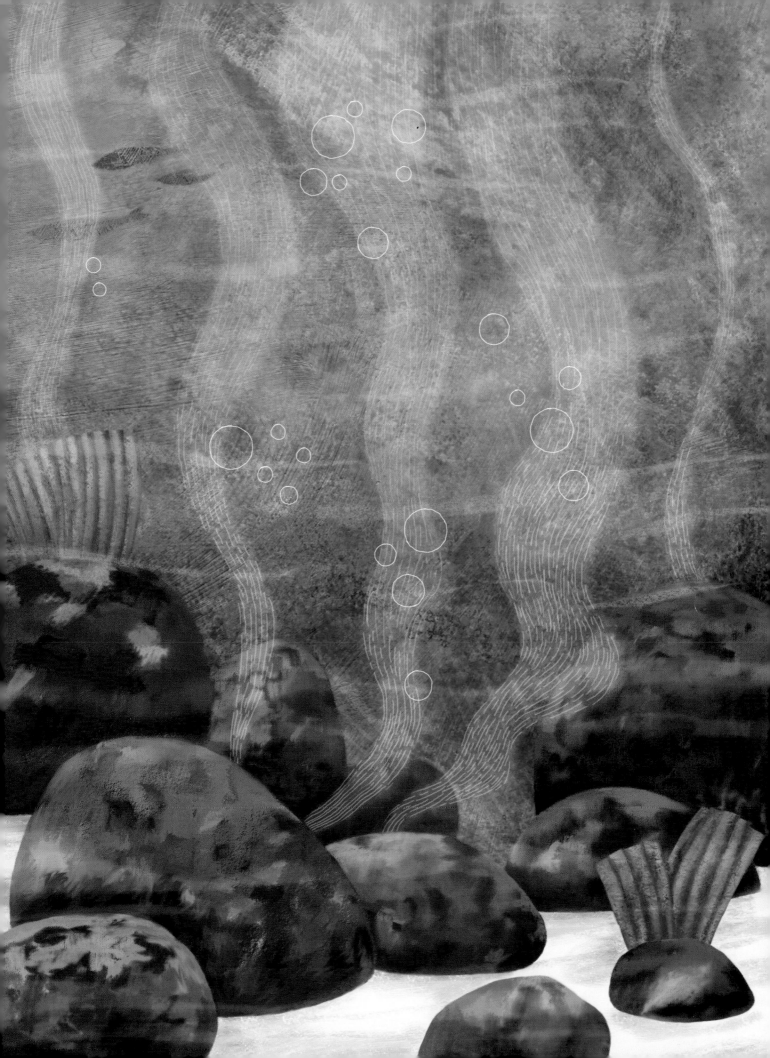

Y de gotita en gotita
voy subiendo a la superficie.
Paso por los poros,
me enredo en las raíces,
subo por las piedras y
viajo por la claridad y la oscuridad.

And drop by tiny drop
I climb to the surface.
I pass through the pores,
get entangled in roots
climb along rocks and
travel through light and darkness.

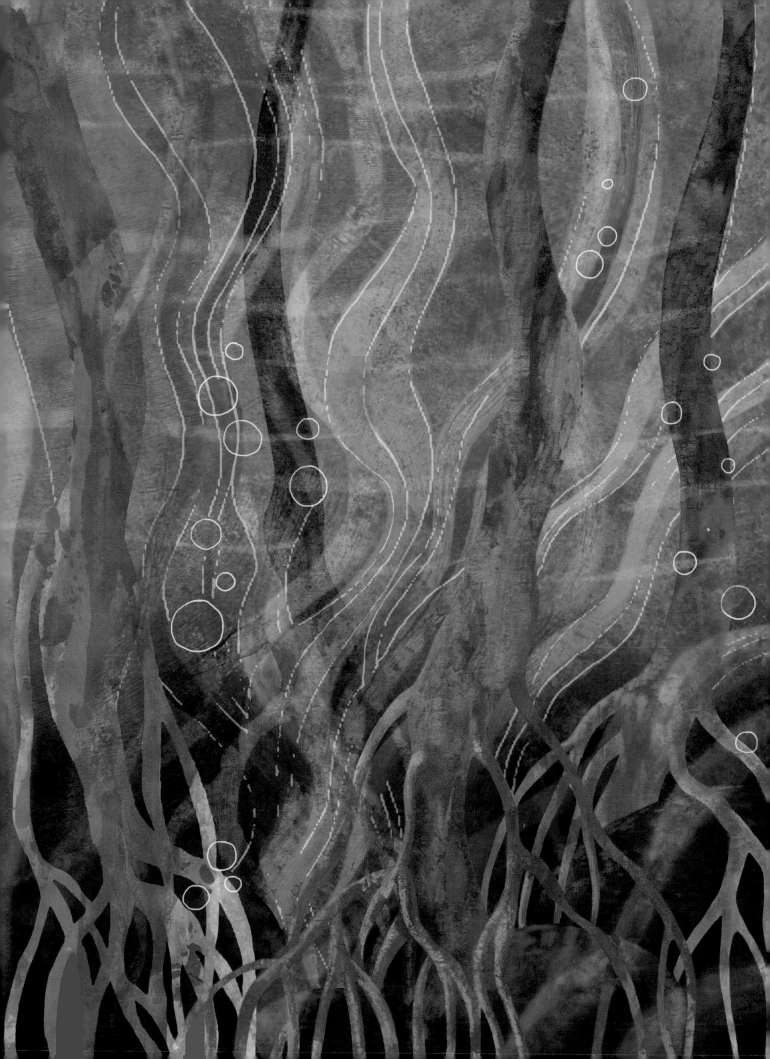

De gotita en gotita
voy subiendo.
Y al llegar a la superficie
me cuelgo a descansar
en las puntas de las hojas,
en las telarañas
o en los pétalos de las flores.

Drop by drop
I climb.
And when I come to the surface
I rest by hanging
on the tips of leaves,
on spider webs
or on flower petals.

Soy Agüita,
un suspiro del rocío de las mañanas.
Agüita,
una canción dulce, tierna y fuerte.

I am Little Water,
a sigh of morning dew.
Little Water,
a sweet, tender and strong song.

Soy Agüita,
y de gotita en gotita . . .

I am Little Water,
and drop by drop . . .

me convierto
en río
en lago
en mar.
De gotita en gotita
subo al cielo.

I become
a river
a lake
an ocean.
Drop by drop
I climb to the sky.

Soy de un color
por la mañana y
de otro color en la tarde.

I am one color
in the morning and
another in the afternoon.

Y luego por la noche
soy de otro.

And then at night
I am another color.

Soy de todos los colores
y no tengo color.
Soy de todos los sabores
y no tengo sabor.
Soy de todas las formas
y no tengo forma.
Soy Agua,
soy Agüita.

I am all colors
and have no color.
I am all flavors
and have no flavor.
I am all shapes
and am shapeless.
I am Water,
I am Little Water.

De gotita en gotita
me convierto en nube.

Drop by drop
I turn into a cloud.

Soy pájaro de agua.
De gotita en gotita
regreso cantando a nuestra Madre Tierra.
Soy Agüita.
Soy vida.

I am a water bird.
Drop by drop
I return singing to our Mother Earth.
I am Little Water.
I am life.

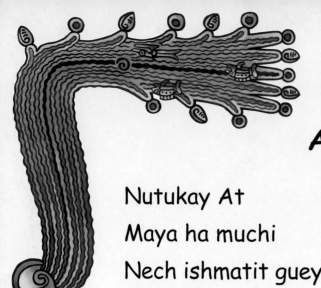

At Achichipiga At

Nutukay At
Maya ha muchi
Nech ishmatit guey atchin

Naja Nugustú
Manéchilguiya
Atchin

Ni nesi tik nemictan
Nunan tal
Gané niwisht nitacuiwa
Ni se achichipiga

Se achichipiga
Gan ajcu se achichipiga
Ni tejcuj ijpack
Ni panu tech nenelguat

Ni tejcuj tét
Ne tejtét
Ni panu gan
Tesu gunyugua

Guan ni panu
Guan gunyugua

Se achichipiga
Guan ajcu se achichipiga

Ni tejcu
Ijpack
Nimughuilana
Gan ni
Musewia tik
Ne itsun
Ne ijiswát
Tik ne
Megat ne tugat

Gan nimusewia
Tik Neshuchit tapantuc

Ni se achichipiga
ijyumigui
Ajwich ipal ne gatapuyagua

Atchin
Takuiwalis supelec huan selec
Huan tesilna

Ni se achichipiga
Ni nimuchigua
Tik ne apan
Tik nejmach at
Tik ne apuyek
Ni se achichipiga
Chujchupi tik chujchupi
Ni tejcu ipal negal

Ipal se tachisca
Gata puyahua
Gatihutak nikpia se tachisca
Ne manga ipal tayua
ni ujce tachisca

Muchi ne tachisca wuan tesu
Nikpia tachisca
Naja ni muchi ne ajuiyach
Tesu nikpia ne ajuiyack

Naja ni muchi guen nechtichiwi
Wuan tesu nikpia nechtichiwi
Maya ni at
Maya ne atchin

Chujchupini tik chujchupi
Ni nimuchigua
mu cuepa misti
ne tutut ipal ne at

Chujchupi tik chujchupi
Ni mucuepa takuiga
Tunan tal
Naja ni atchin
Naja ni tayulcuitiya.

Photo credit: Teresa Kennett

Jorge Tetl Argueta es un galardonado escritor de libros infantiles y de poesía para niños. También es el fundador de La Biblioteca de Los Sueños/Library of Dreams en El Salvador. Ha recibido el International Latino Book Award, el Américas Book Award, el NAPPA Gold Award y el Independent Publisher Book Award en la categoría de Ficción Multicultural para Jóvenes y el Lee Bennet Poetry Award. Sus libros han sido incluidos en la Américas Award Commended List, el USBBY Outstanding International Books Honors List, *Kirkus Reviews* Best Children's Books y el Cooperative Children's Book Center Choices. Indígena salvadoreño de origen pipil-nahua, Jorge pasó gran parte de su vida en El Salvador rural. Ahora vive en San Francisco, California, donde es Poeta Laureado de las Bibliotecas Públicas de San Francisco.

Jorge Tetl Argueta is an award-winning author of picture books and poetry for young children. He is also the founder of La Biblioteca de los Sueños/Library of Dreams in El Salvador. He has won the International Latino Book Award, the Américas Book Award, the NAPPA Gold Award, the Independent Publisher Book Award for Multicultural Fiction for Juveniles and the Lee Bennet Poetry Award. His books have also been named to the Américas Award Commended List, the USBBY Outstanding International Books Honor List, *Kirkus Reviews* Best Children's Books and the Cooperative Children's Book Center Choices. A native Salvadoran and Pipil-Nahua Indian, Jorge spent much of his life in rural El Salvador. He now lives in San Francisco, California, where he is Poet Laureate of the San Francisco Public Libraries.

Felipe Ugalde Alcántara nació en la ciudad de México en 1962 y estudió Comunicación Gráfica en la Escuela Nacional de Arte en la Universidad Nacional de México. Ha trabajado como ilustrador y diseñador de libros infantiles, libros de texto y juegos educacionales para prestigiosas casas editoriales por veinticinco años. También ha dictado talleres de ilustración para niños y profesionales, y ha participado en varias exhibiciones en México y en el extranjero. Ha sido galardonado con premios de ilustración en España, México y Japón. Ugalde Alcántara ilustró *Mother Fox and Mr. Coyote/Mamá Zorra y Don Coyote* y *Little Crow to the Rescue/El Cuervito al rescate* para Piñata Books.

Felipe Ugalde Alcántara was born in Mexico City and studied Graphic Communication at the National University of Mexico's School of Art. He has been an illustrator and designer for children's books, textbooks and educational games for twenty-five years. He has taught illustration workshops for children and professionals and participated in several exhibitions in Mexico and abroad. He has received illustration awards in Spain, Mexico and Japan. Ugalde Alcántara illustrated *Mother Fox and Mr. Coyote/Mamá Zorra y Don Coyote* and *Little Crow to the Rescue/El Cuervito al rescate* for Piñata Books.